D1408350

A bilingual alphabet book

The Lion in the Lake
Le lion dans le lac

Un abécédaire bilingue

■

Sheldon Oberman

with illustrations by/illustré par

Scott Barham

1988

Peguis Publishers Limited, Winnipeg, Manitoba, Canada

Copyright © text Sheldon Oberman, 1988
Copyright © illustrations Scott Barham, 1988

Canadian Cataloguing in Publication Data

Oberman, Sheldon.

The lion in the lake

Text in English and French.
ISBN 0-920541-36-4

1. Readers (Primary). 2. English language – Alphabet – Juvenile literature.
3. French language – Readers (Primary).*
4. French language – Alphabet – Juvenile literature.
I. Barham, Scott, 1955-
II. Title. III. Title: Le lion dans le lac.

PE1119.023 1988   j428.6   C88-098151-2 E

Book design by Pat Stanton
Printed in Canada by Hignell Printing Limited

Texte copyright © 1988 par Sheldon Oberman
Illustrations copyright © 1988 par Scott Barham

Données de catalogage avant publication (Canada)

Oberman, Sheldon.

The lion in the lake

Texte en anglais et en français.
ISBN 0-920541-36-4

1. Abécédaires anglais. 2. Anglais (Langue) – Alphabet – Ouvrages pour la jeunesse.
3. Abécédaires.
4. Français (Langue) – Alphabet – Ouvrages pour la jeunesse.
I. Barham, Scott, 1955-
II. Titre. III. Titre: Le lion dans le lac.

PE1119.023 1988   j428.6   C88-098151-2 F

Dessein du livre par Pat Stanton
Imprimé au Canada par Hignell Printing Limited

Aa

**The alligator and
the airplane**

■

**L'alligator et
l'avion**

Bb

**The baby
in the boat**

■

**Le bébé
dans le bateau**

The cat and the canaries

Le chat et les canaris

Dd

**The dragon and
the deer**

■

**Le dragon et
le daim**

Ee

**An elephant
goes to school**

**Un éléphant
va à l'école**

Ff

A flower in the
forest

▪

Une fleur dans la
forêt

Gg

**A gymnast and
a giraffe**

■

**Un gymnaste et
une girafe**

Hh

A helicopter
near the hospital

.

Un hélicoptère
près de l'hôpital

Ii

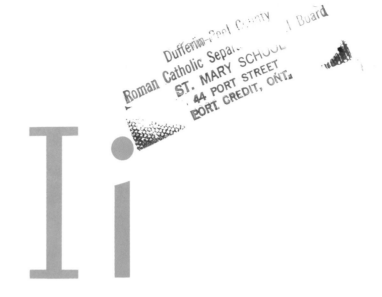

**An igloo
on an island**

**Un igloo
sur une île**

Jj

A juggler in the jungle

Un jongleur dans la jungle

Kk

**Kangaroos race
five kilometers**

.

**Des kangourous courant
cinq kilomètres**

Ll

**The lion
in the lake**

**Le lion
dans le lac**

The magician on the mountain

■

Le magicien sur la montagne

Nn

**The nose
in a nest**

∎

**Le nez
dans un nid**

**An ogre eats
onions and oranges**

■

**Un ogre mange des
oignons et des oranges**

Pp

**The pirate and
the parrots**

■

**Le pirate et
les perroquets**

Qq

A quartet in
Quebec

∎

Un quartette à
Québec

Rr

**The raccoon
and the rose**

■

**Le raton-laveur
et la rose**

Ss

The snake in the sun

■

Le serpent au soleil

Tt

The turtle
and the train

•

La tortue
et le train

Uu

**The unicorn likes
the uniform**

**L'unicorne aime
l'uniforme**

Vv

**The violin and
the volcano**

■

**Le violon et
le volcan**

Ww

A wagon
near a wigwam

■

Un wagon
près d'un wigwam

Xenia and her xylophone

•

Xenia et son xylophone

**The yak and
the yoyo**

■

**Le yack et
le yoyo**

Zz

**The zebra leaves
the zoo**

■

**Le zèbre quitte
le zoo**

Sheldon Oberman was born in Winnipeg, Manitoba and earned Arts and Education degrees from the University of Manitoba and an M.A. in English from the University of Jerusalem. His award-winning poetry, fiction, and drama have been widely published and performed. He has written lyrics for many Canadian children's performers and his title song for "The Polka-Dot Pony" (with Fred Penner) was nominated for a Juno Award. Sheldon teaches high school Drama, English and Journalism and continues his prolific freelance writing.

Sheldon Oberman est né à Winnipeg, Manitoba. Il a obtenu ses diplômes en arts et en éducation à l'Université du Manitoba et sa maîtrise d'anglais à l'Université de Jérusalem. Sa poésie et ses oeuvres de fiction et de théâtre ont remporté plusieurs prix et ont souvent été publiés ou mis en scène. Parolier de nombreux chanteurs canadiens pour enfants, il a écrit "The Polka-Dot Pony" qu'a fait connaître Fred Penner dans son microsillon du même titre. Cette chanson lui a valu une nomination au prix Juno. Tout en poursuivant ses activités d'écrivain, Sheldon enseigne le théâtre, l'anglais et le journalisme au niveau secondaire.

Scott Barham was born in Monominto, Manitoba and graduated from the University of Manitoba's School of Fine Arts. His multi-media visual art and clay sculptures have been shown extensively and his quirky cartoons are a regular feature of many Canadian publications. Scott is currently working on publishing projects in Canada and Europe as well as commissions for both ceramic and visual art.

Scott Barham est né à Monominto, Manitoba, et a obtenu son diplôme des Beaux-Arts à l'Université du Manitoba. Ses oeuvres visuelles faites avec une variété de matériels, ainsi que ses sculptures en céramique, ont figuré dans de nombreuses expositions, et on voit régulièrement ses caricatures excentriques dans les pages de plusieurs revues canadiennes. À l'heure actuelle, Scott travaille sur divers projets qui seront publiés au Canada et en Europe et exécute des commandes de céramiques et d'oeuvres d'art visuel.